This book belongs to:

_____

_____

_____

First published 2021 by Walker Books Ltd
87 Vauxhall Walk, London SE11 5HJ

2 4 6 8 10 9 7 5 3 1

© 1990–2021 Lucy Cousins
Lucy Cousins font © 1990–2021 Lucy Cousins

The author/illustrator has asserted her moral rights

Maisy™. Maisy is a trademark of Walker Books Ltd, London

Printed in China

British Library Cataloguing in Publication Data:
a catalogue record for this book is
available from the British Library.

ISBN 978-1-4063-9511-2

www.walker.co.uk

Maisy's Surprise Birthday Party

Lucy Cousins

WALKER BOOKS

AND SUBSIDIARIES

LONDON · BOSTON · SYDNEY · AUCKLAND

It's a beautiful, sunny day, and Maisy has woken up very early.

Today is her birthday. Hooray!

Maisy goes
downstairs
to make
breakfast.

Pancakes – yum, yum, what a lovely birthday treat!

Maisy puts on her favourite outfit, then goes to check the post.

There's only one letter!

It's from Charley. He wants her to come to his house straight away.

When Maisy gets to Charley's house, the curtains are closed but the door is open.

How strange!

Maisy knocks and tiptoes inside.

It's very dark inside
the house.

"Hello?" Maisy calls.

She reaches for the light
switch -

CLICK!

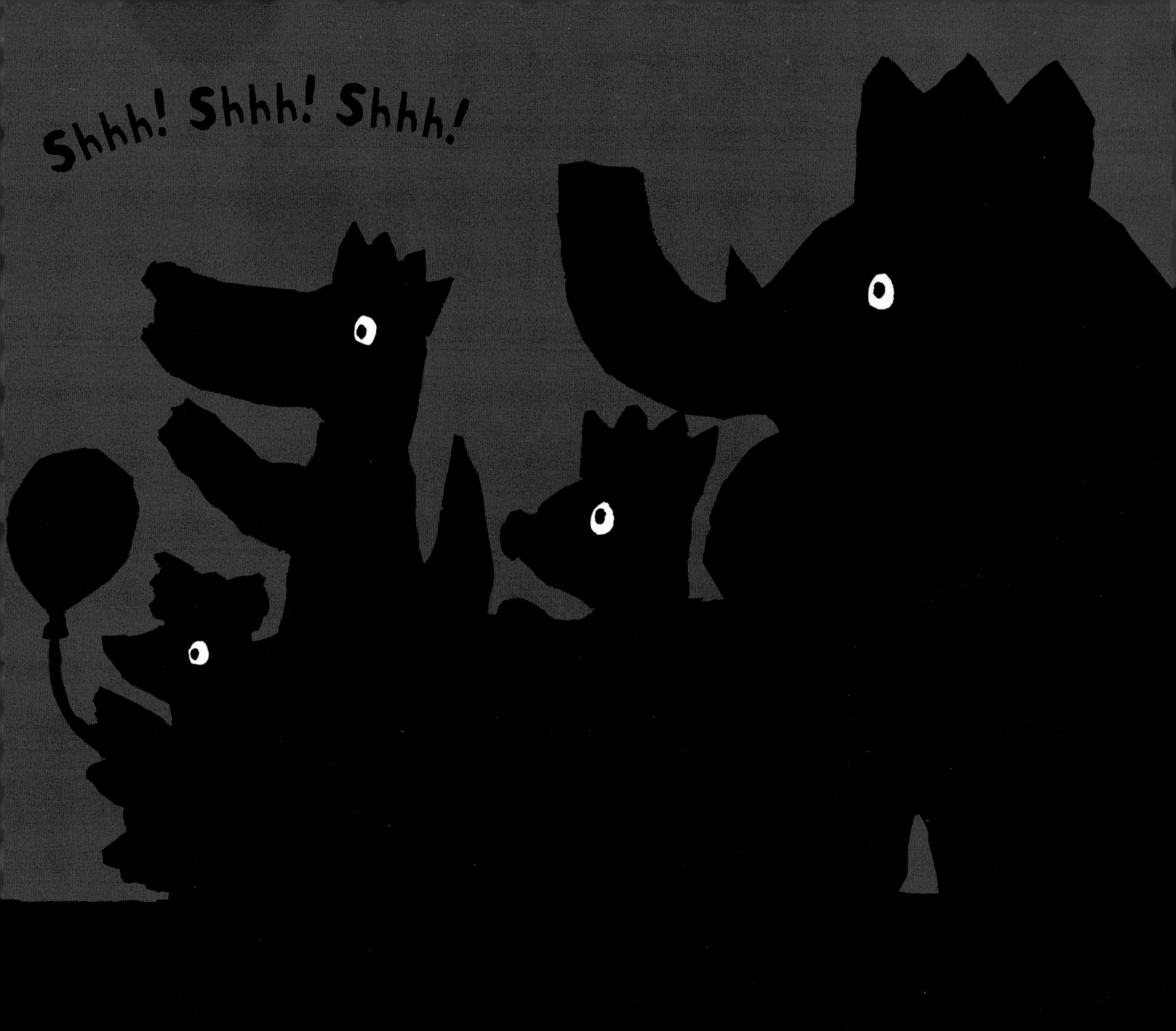
Shhh! Shhh! Shhh!

Maisy's friends are here to celebrate
and they've brought PRESENTS!

Lucky, lucky Maisy!

Each friend has brought
something special for her.
She opens her presents
and looks at her cards.

"Thank you so much, everyone!"
Maisy says.

Everyone gets to
play with Maisy's
new toys.

"Wheee!"

"Once
upon a
time..."

"I know where this piece goes!"

Shake-jingle-jingle!

Then it's time for party games.
Everyone else finds a place to hide
while Maisy counts to ten.

Can you see who's hiding where?

After Maisy has found everyone, they all gather at the table for a party tea.

There is juice, fruit, fairy cakes and
lots of cheese — Maisy's favourite!

Suddenly the lights
are turned off again.

What do you think is
going to happen?

Maisy's friends have made her a birthday cake!

Maisy closes her eyes and makes a wish. This has been the best surprise birthday party ever!